HAPPINESS

Honor Head

W
FRANKLIN WATTS
LONDON • SYDNEY

Published in paperback in Great Britain in 2020
by The Watts Publishing Group
© The Watts Publishing Group 2020

Managing editor: Victoria Brooker
Design: Sophie Burdess

Image Credits: Shutterstock – all images Good Studio
apart from Iveta Angelova & Ollikeballoon
graphic elements throughout;
LOLE 20l, ONYX 21 tc, Zarian 7c.

Every attempt has been made to clear copyright.
Should there be any inadvertent omission
please apply to the publisher for rectification.

ISBN: 978 1 4451 6992 7 (hbk)
ISBN: 978 1 4451 6993 4 (pbk)

Printed in China

Franklin Watts
An imprint of
Hachette Children's Group
Part of the Watts Publishing Group
Carmelite House
50 Victoria Embankment
London EC4Y 0DZ
An Hachette UK Company
www.hachette.co.uk
www.franklinwatts.co.uk

The website addresses (URLs) included in this book
were valid at the time of going to press.
However, it is possible that contents or addresses may
have changed since the publication of this book.
No responsibility for any such changes can be accepted
by either the author or the Publisher.

CONTENTS

HOW TO BE HAPPY

Happiness means different things to different people,
such as laughing with friends or relaxing at home.

PLAYING
FOOTBALL WITH
MY BEST MATES

BEING WITH
MY FAMILY

GETTING MY
HOMEWORK DONE
ON TIME

WALKING
MY DOG

SEEING A
RAINBOW

HELPING
GRANNY WITH
HER SHOPPING

SOME THINGS ABOUT HAPPINESS

You can try, but it's pretty impossible to be happy all the time.
Everyone has moments when they feel unhappy. And that's fine.
But you can do things to try and change this.

Being happy is about...

being interested in life,
getting involved,
enjoying being with
friends and family,
being kind
and caring.

HAPPY

Get started on the happiness journey now.
This books has loads of ideas, tips and advice
on how to enjoy your life.

1. LEARN TO LOVE LEARNING

Trying new foods, meeting new people, seeing new places, learning new skills ... all these are different experiences that make life interesting and exciting.

NEW IS THE NEW YOU!

WHY DOES LEARNING AND DOING NEW THINGS MATTER?

You can **SHARE** your skills and interests.

Learning a new skill boosts your self-esteem so you can **FEEL GREAT ABOUT YOURSELF.**

If you're absorbed in something you really enjoy, there is **NO TIME TO WORRY** about other things.

Joining new groups and clubs is a brilliant way to **MAKE FRIENDS.**

Learning something active **KEEPS YOUR BODY FIT** too.

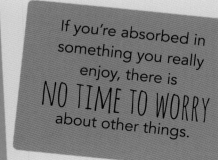

Being curious and interested in everything around you **KEEPS YOUR BRAIN ACTIVE AND HEALTHY.**

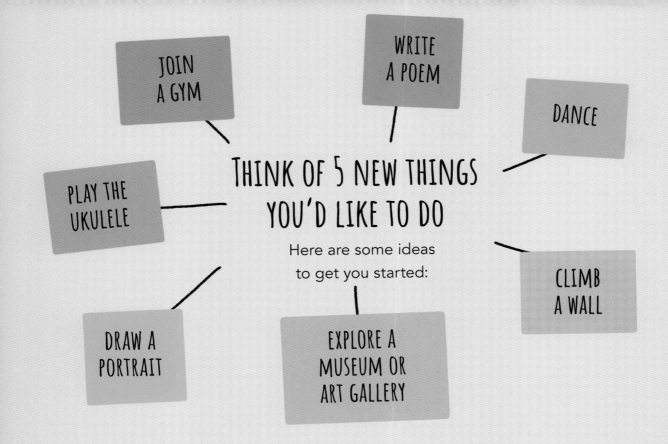

JOIN A GYM

WRITE A POEM

DANCE

PLAY THE UKULELE

Think of 5 new things you'd like to do

Here are some ideas to get you started:

DRAW A PORTRAIT

EXPLORE A MUSEUM OR ART GALLERY

CLIMB A WALL

 # What if I can't do it?

What if you **can** do it? What if you discover you are the very best at dancing, climbing walls or writing poetry? And so what if you're not! There's nothing that says you have to be brilliant at everything... if you enjoy doing something, that's all that matters.

GIVE IT A GO – OR YOU'LL NEVER KNOW!

DO IT AND SURPRISE YOURSELF!

LIVE, LEARN, LOVE LIFE!

2. TALK

When you feel sad, anxious, worried
or scared about something
it will help to talk about it.

I LOVE HELPING MY FRIENDS BY LISTENING TO THEM. THEY DO THE SAME FOR ME.

WHEN I TALK TO MY FRIENDS OR FAMILY, I DON'T FEEL SO ALONE.

SHARING MY ANXIETIES MAKES THEM SEEM LESS SCARY.

I FEEL LESS STRESSED TALKING WITH MY MATES

TALKING ABOUT MY PROBLEMS AND WORRIES HELPS ME TO UNDERSTAND WHY I FEEL THE WAY I DO.

TALKING TIPS

TALKING ABOUT A PROBLEM DOESN'T MAKE YOU WEAK OR SILLY. IT IS A BRAVE AND SENSIBLE THING TO DO.

Talk where you won't
be disturbed.

Joining a safe online forum
or chat room can help you
share your problems with
others who feel the same.
Never give away
personal details.

Feeling nervous?
WRITE IT DOWN.
Let the other person
read it and then talk.

LISTENING TIPS

To talk to a busy family member,
CHOOSE A TIME AND PLACE
when you both feel calm and focused.

Don't share what you are told unless you have permission.

DON'T JUDGE

DON'T INTERRUPT

IT TAKES COURAGE TO TALK ...

...AND PATIENCE TO LISTEN!

ALL DONE TALKING...

...SHOW SOMEONE YOU CARE. HAVE A HUG!

3. EXERCISE

Exercise and keeping active is important to your physical and mental health.

When you exercise, your brain releases chemicals that make you feel happier and able to cope with everyday stress.

Regular aerobic exercise keeps your heart and lungs healthy and makes your bones stronger, too. Aerobic exercise is any activity that makes your heart work harder and makes you breathless.

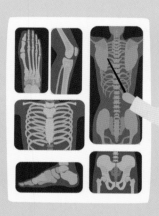

Sport is a great way to spend time with friends. Being active helps to make you feel good about yourself. You will feel really proud of how strong and fit you are.

Some activities help you to stay supple and bendy.

Some exercises help to build up your muscles and make you strong.

Choose the right activity for you:

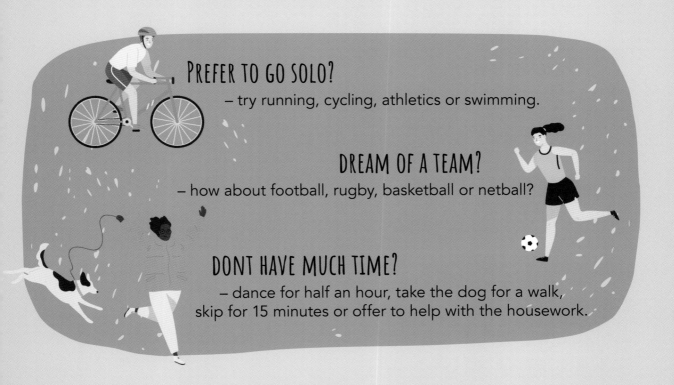

Prefer to go solo?
— try running, cycling, athletics or swimming.

Dream of a team?
— how about football, rugby, basketball or netball?

Dont have much time?
— dance for half an hour, take the dog for a walk, skip for 15 minutes or offer to help with the housework.

And being active helps you sleep better. Sweet dreams!

4. APPRECIATE THE SIMPLE THINGS IN LIFE

Sometimes, life can get really busy and stressful.
Slow down… look around, take a breath
and notice the simple things of your day.

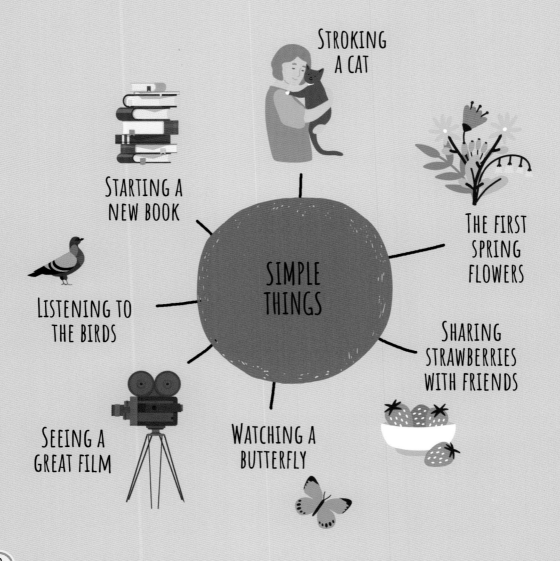

STROKING A CAT

STARTING A NEW BOOK

THE FIRST SPRING FLOWERS

SIMPLE THINGS

LISTENING TO THE BIRDS

SHARING STRAWBERRIES WITH FRIENDS

SEEING A GREAT FILM

WATCHING A BUTTERFLY

It doesn't take much to make someone happy...

And when we make others happy we feel happy too.

• Make a call. Phone someone you haven't spoken to for a while. It could be your granny, an aunt or your best friend who moved away.

• Give someone a compliment.

• Offer to help at home with the chores. Helping others will make you feel good.

Make yourself happy.

Be grateful for everything you have...
including being the special and amazing person you are.

Try to find one thing every day to be thankful for

• amazing family (well, sometimes!)

• great friends

• the best pet in the world

• being healthy and strong

• being able to learn new things.

5. RELAX

When it all gets too much and the stresses start piling up,
try these techniques to help you relax mentally and physically.

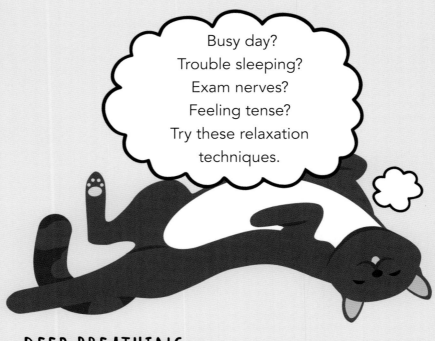

Busy day?
Trouble sleeping?
Exam nerves?
Feeling tense?
Try these relaxation
techniques.

DEEP BREATHING

- Lie down or sit and close your eyes.

- Take in a deep, slow breath through your nose.

- Breathe out slowly through your mouth.

- Try this up to ten times twice a day.

RELEASE TENSION

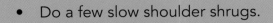

- Do a few slow shoulder shrugs.

- Then on an in breath, make a tight fist.

- On the out breath release your hand and stretch out your fingers.

- Imagine the tension flowing out through your fingertips.

EMPTY YOUR MIND

- Find a quiet spot to sit or stand.

- Banish any worries for 5 minutes.

- Deep breathe and focus on your surroundings instead.

- What can you hear? See? Smell?

- Let your body relax, your shoulders drop down and your arms become loose.

MOVE IT!

Dancing, kicking around a ball or going for a run can help you unwind after a stressful day.

SMILE!

Smiling helps you relax and makes others feel better, too.

6. DIGITAL DOWNTIME

Taking a break from your digital devices gives you a chance to try something new and meet up with people face-to-face.

BREAK FREE FROM THE SCREEN

BY HAVING REGULAR SCREEN BREAKS YOU WILL:

- sleep better
- have time to talk to friends face-to-face
- improve your posture and all-round health
- feel less stressed
- have more time to try new things.

MAKE NON-SCREEN TIME FUN

Have a regular dance, cook or book club get together with your best mates.

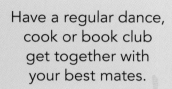

Try a screen-free sleepover – tell spooky stories by torchlight, make pizzas and fruit kebabs or listen to your favourite music.

Go to the park.

Have a competition with your family – who can stay screen-free the longest in one day or a week!

Think about creative screen-free evenings – draw and paint, craft, start writing a novel, put on a play, organise a fashion show, form a band, write music.

Send a message that you are going to be offline for a while. Messages from friends will still be there when you go back. Instead of scrolling through photos and messages showing other people having fun, you can be having fun yourself!

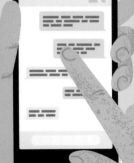

DITCH THE FOMO AND MAKE YOUR OWN GOOD TIMES!

7. GIVE

Giving makes others happy and makes you feel good about yourself. It's a win-win situation!

Help out more at home.

Make a memory book with photos for someone you don't see often.

Use your pocket money to buy one item a week for the food bank.

WAYS TO GIVE

Hold doors open for people.

Sort out old clothes, books and toys for charity shops.

Visit a family member or friend who might be feeling lonely.

Give up your seat on a crowded bus or train.

Make friends with classmates who look sad or left out.

VOLUNTEER

FUNDRAISE!

FIND A CAUSE YOU CARE ABOUT AND RAISE MONEY FOR IT.

Check out local charities looking for volunteers. Try the library, local newspaper or go online.

Have a bake sale.

Help local groups collect litter.

Make some craft stuff to sell.

Have a garage sale of your old toys and books.

8. EAT WELL

Ready-prepared meals, sugary snacks and takeaways can make you feel slow and grumpy. Eat fresh food and make your own meals as much as you can.

SHOPPING LIST

Fruit: fresh or tinned but not in heavy syrup

Vegetables: fresh, frozen or tinned

Fresh meat and fish

Brown or wholegrain pasta, bread, potatoes and rice

~~Ready meals, crisps and salted nuts, burger and chips.~~

Pop some fruit or veggie sticks into your lunch box for a mid-morning snack. Try oat cakes, rice cakes and sticks of carrot, celery and cucumber with a houmous dip for a healthy and tasty snack.

For sandwiches and rolls try BROWN bread instead of white.

HEALTHY DINNER IS SERVED!

At home, or when you are out, choose healthy options, such as steamed veggies instead of boiled, grilled chicken instead of fried, boiled or jacket potatoes instead of chips.

MASTER COOK

Have a competition with your friends or family.
Who can make the best salads and fruit kebabs?
Use a colourful range of fruit and vegetables.

carrots	apples
radishes	pears
tomatoes	melon
cucumber	bananas
sweetcorn	oranges
celery	grapes
beetroot	strawberries
courgettes	plums

SPECIAL TREATS

Have these only as a special treat – ice cream, cakes, biscuits, sweets, chocolate.

9. DRINK WATER

Your body is up to 60 per cent water!
You need water to keep you mentally alert and physically fit.

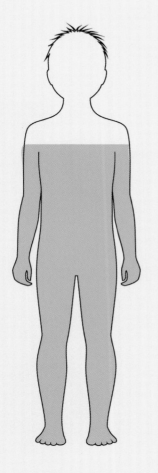

WHY WATER?

Why can't I have my favourite drinks?
Here's why…

12 oz can of coke = 8 teaspoons sugar

glass of apple juice = 7 teaspoons sugar

glass of water = empty teaspoons

Even fruit
drinks that say
NO ADDED SUGAR
contain lots of
sugar from the
natural fruit.

AIM TO DRINK UP TO 6 GLASSES OF WATER A DAY

TO HELP YOU DO THIS:

Drink a glass of water when you get up.

WATER

Buy yourself a fabulous water bottle and sip from it during the day.

Drink a glass with each meal.

HEY, WHAT ABOUT ABOUT ME?

MILK

Yes, milk is good for you too, but water is best – it's free and only a tap away!

10. GET OUTDOORS

Research has shown that spending time in the fresh air
and getting to know nature improves our moods.
Keeping active outside can also keep us fit.
Get together with family and friends and
explore the great outdoors today!

TAKE A WALK
AND LISTEN
TO THE BIRDS

FLY A KITE

BUILD A
SNOWMAN

GROW HERBS
IN POTS

DRAW FLOWERS
AND TREES

GO CAMPING

VISIT LOCAL
MARSHLANDS

SIT UNDER A
TREE AND READ

SWIM IN
THE SEA

LEARN HOW TO
USE A COMPASS

Whatever the weather, get outside and have fun – don't forget to take your water bottle with you. If it is hot, always wear sunscreen.

GO BUY A BOOK OF BIRDS AND SEE HOW MANY YOU CAN SPOT

PLAY FOOTBALL, RUGBY OR ROUNDERS

HAVE A PICNIC

HAVE A NATURE PHOTO EXHIBITION WITH YOUR MATES – NO SELFIES ALLOWED!

RIDE A BIKE

SKATEBOARD

FIND AN OPEN AIR SWIMMING POOL OR LIDO

GO ROWING

GO ROCKPOOLING

TRY PADDLEBOARDING

LEARN THE NAMES OF TREES

11. SLEEP WELL

While you sleep, your brain and body have lots of work to do. Getting about 9.5 hours of sleep a night gives them the time to do it.

As you sleep your brain processes everything that has happened during the day.

It files away what you thought, said, did, learnt and felt.

It makes memories.

The cells and neurons in your brain are renewed to improve concentration and memory.

Getting enough sleep means you are less likely to feel grumpy, irritable or moody the next day.

Sleep helps your body to grow and heal.

You will enjoy your day more.

FOR A GOOD NIGHT'S SLEEP...

Get into a routine and go to bed at the same time every night.

WRITE DOWN ANYTHING THAT IS WORRYING YOU. PUT THE PAPER AWAY TO DEAL WITH IN THE MORNING. THINGS ALWAYS LOOK BETTER IN THE MORNING.

Turn off your computer and phone an hour before sleeping.

Tossing and turning all night? Try breathing deeply in and out. Focus on relaxing each part of your body starting with your toes.

Make sure you are not too hot or too cold.

Exercising during the day will help you sleep better. But not just before bedtime!

Read your favourite book.

12. ASK FOR HELP

Everyone needs help at times for lots of different reasons.
Sometimes you need to be brave and admit it's time to ask for help.
Learn to recognise when you should ask for help…

HELP!
I can't cope
anymore.

HELP!
I feel sad
all the time.

HELP!
I feel lonely.

HELP!
I feel angry
all the time.

HELP!
Someone is
hurting me.

HELP!
I am so scared
of bad things
happening.

HELP!
My eating
habits have
become
really unhealthy.

HELP!
I feel sick
and achey
all the time.

HELP!
I feel like
a failure.

HELP!
I cry
all the time.

HELP!
I feel like I want
to harm myself.

HELP!
I just want
to be by
myself the
whole time.

HELP!
I can't sleep
at night.

TURN HERE TO FIND OUT
WHERE YOU CAN GET HELP...

WHERE TO GET HELP

First off, try to talk to someone about how you feel.
If there is no one you want to talk to, there are lots of
places online that can help you. Chat rooms and forums are great
for talking to people who feel the same way as you do and may have
had similar experiences. However, never share personal details with any
one, no matter how genuine they seem. Never meet up with strangers.

Telephone helplines are places where you can talk to someone who
is specially trained to understand what you are going through.
They won't judge you or make you do anything you don't want to do.
You don't have to be embarrassed or ashamed or silly about what you
tell them. They will be understanding, kind and supportive.

www.childline.org.uk/info-advice/your-feelings/mental-health
Message or call the 24-hour helpline
for advice or someone who'll just listen.
The helpline is 0800 1111

https://papyrus-uk.org
A place to go if you have thoughts
about harming yourself or suicide.
HopelineUK 0800 068 41 41

www.samaritans.org
A place where anyone can go for
advice and comfort.
The helpline is 08457 90 90 90

www.sane.org/get-help
Help and support for anyone affected
by mental and emotional issues.
The helpline is 0300 304 7000

www.supportline.org.uk
A charity giving emotional
support to young people.
The helpline is 01708 765200

kidshealth.org/en/kids/feeling
Advice on managing emotions.

www.youngminds.org.uk
Advice for young people
experiencing bullying, stress
and mental or emotional anxieties.

www.brainline.org/article/who-me-self-esteem-people-disabilities
How to boost self-esteem
regardless of disabilities.

SHOUT!
A text-only 24/7 helpline for anyone suffering from
emotional and mental issues or going through a crisis.
Text 85258 and a trained volunteer will be there to help.

Or settle down with a book...

**Hello Happy! Mindful Kids:
An activity book for young people who
sometimes feel sad or angry**
by Stephanie Clarkson and Katie Abey,
Studio Press, 2017

Create Your Own Happy
by Penny Alexander and Becky Goddard-Hill,
Collins, 2018

GLOSSARY

aerobic exercise that makes your heart beat faster

anxiety feeling worried and nervous

cells tiny parts of the body that can only be seen with a microscope

compliment to praise someone; to say something nice about how someone looks or behaves

concentration to really focus on something

FOMO acronym for 'Fear Of Missing Out'

irritable easily annoyed or snappy

neurons types of cells that send information around your body using chemical and electrical signals

posture the way you hold your body when you move

stress feeling physically or mentally tense and worried

tension mental, physical or emotional stress or strain

unwind relax, feel less tense or stressed

volunteers people who do something for free in their own time

INDEX